Deception

Mafia Ties #1

Fiona Davenport

Love is not blind,

it sees more not less;

but because it sees more,

it chooses to see less.

- Unknown -

Copyright

© 2016 Fiona Davenport
All rights reserved.
Edited by PREMA Romance Editing.

All rights reserved. No part of this book may be reproduced or transmitted in any form or by any means, electronic or mechanical, including photocopying, recording, or by any information storage and retrieval system, without permission in writing. For permission requests, please send your email request to authorfionadavenport@yahoo.com.

This is a work of fiction. Names, characters, places and incidents are the product of the author's imagination or are used factiously, and any resemblance to any actual persons or living or dead, events or locales are entirely coincidental.

The author acknowledges the trademark status and trademark owners of various products referenced in this work of fiction, which have been used without permission. The publication/ Use of these trademarks is not authorized, associated with, or sponsored by the trademark owner.

Chapter 1

Anna

"Good morning, Anna," the recruiter at the Manhattan nanny agency greeted me, waving towards the chair in front of her desk. "You look lovely this morning."

"Thank you." My reply was faint. I might look nice on the outside, but I was a mess on the inside as I sat down across from her. I'd dressed with extra care this morning because I needed the boost in confidence. I'd hoped to have been placed with a family by now, but each of my interviews had been worse than the next.

The first family's home had been a disaster and they'd fully expected the nanny to be the one to clean it. The second family's children were holy terrors who'd managed to scare off three nannies in two weeks. My third interview was a couple days ago and had been horrible.

The mother hadn't been able to make the appointment due to a work commitment and the father made it quite clear he expected to receive special attention if he hired me. It had been enough to make me seriously reconsider if I was cut out to be a nanny.

"I'm sorry things haven't gone smoothly for you so far. Matching a nanny with a family isn't always an easy task, but I'm sure we'll be able to find something suitable for you."

At least one of us was sure. "I hate to admit it, but I was thinking maybe this was a sign that I should try to do something else instead."

She cocked her head and studied me a moment, most likely trying to gauge how serious I was about giving up. "Are you willing to give me one more chance?"

My hands twisted in my lap, toying with the edge of the cardigan sweater I'd paired with a sundress to make it more appropriate for a visit to her office. "Maybe."

With a nod, she lifted a manila folder off the top of a stack and flipped it open. She scanned it quickly before flashing me a smile. "I think this might be perfect for you. The girl is six years old and has had health issues, almost from birth. Because of her illness, it's harder to find a nanny to accept the position. Your schooling could be put to good use."

My heart strings tugged, even though I knew my one year studying to become a physical therapy assistant wouldn't be much help when it came to caring for a sick child.

"Her grandmother has been caring for her, but she isn't able to keep up with her any longer—not because of Sophia's health issues, but because she's had a health scare of her own. Her dad came to us several weeks ago, but so far we haven't had any luck matching them with a nanny."

I noticed a glaring omission in her description of the family. "What about her mom?"

She rifled through the papers in the folder before answering. "I can only assume she isn't a part of her daughter's life since there was no mention of her in the information provided."

"After what happened on the last interview, I'd really prefer a position with a family, with a wife who will be around a lot. Not a single dad."

She closed the folder and leaned towards me, lowering her voice. "I was lucky enough to meet with Mr. DeLuca in person. I don't think I've ever met a more gorgeous man. Trust me when I tell you that he has no need to take advantage of an employee. Not only is he sexy, he has money too. You're a pretty girl, but I'm sure he has women throwing themselves at him left and right."

"Okay," I sighed, feeling like she'd put me in my place.

I was a nanny who couldn't find a charge, and this little girl sounded like she couldn't find a nanny. Maybe it was meant to be. Besides, if the interview didn't go well, I could just throw in the towel and think of something else to do. Really, what was the worst thing that could happen?

An hour later, I was untying my cardigan from around my waist so I could put it back on before knocking on the door of the impressive brownstone, on the upper west side, in front of me. Although my cream and pink striped sundress was flattering, it was hardly appropriate for an interview with its spaghetti straps and low neckline. All of which I wasn't able to cover up with my sweater before the door flew open.

A tall, dark-haired man with a neatly trimmed beard stood in front of me. His black, button-down shirt was drawn tautly across his muscular chest because one of his arms was pulled behind his back as he held the door. His dark gaze swept over me from head to toe, and I felt my skin heat in response to the flare in his eyes as they landed on my chest. He whispered something under his breath. It sounded like it might have been Italian. I hurriedly put my sweater on and buttoned it up, well aware that his gaze remained on me the entire time. When I lifted my head once again, his lips were tilted up in a smirk that somehow made him even more attractive.

"Anna Martin, I presume?" His voice was deep and slightly rough, a perfect match for his looks.

"Yes," I replied, my voice quivering at the end as he lifted my hand to his lips instead of shaking it.

"I'm Niccolo DeLuca. Nic," he introduced himself, tugging me into the house and keeping possession of my hand to lead me into an office in the back.

I should have known, but he was much younger than I had expected. Most likely still in his early twenties. Holy heck, the recruiter wasn't kidding when she said he was hot. If anything, she'd understated it. After my experience with the dad at my third interview, I'd been understandably nervous about the idea of working for a single dad. But if Nic DeLuca wanted to sexually harass me, I wasn't sure I'd complain.

"Please have a seat," he gestured to a small, brown leather couch.

After he helped me get settled, he dropped down onto the matching chair which was diagonally opposite from me. His legs were long enough that my bare calf brushed against his dress pants.

"Thank you for agreeing to meet with me on such short notice."

"It wasn't a problem at all. I had a meeting at the agency this morning, so I was already out and about anyway," I assured him.

"My mother fell and broke her arm about a month ago, and it brought my attention to just how much she does for Sophia and me. Unfortunately, her doctor has decided she needs surgery because the break isn't healing the way he'd like. So, the need to find a suitable nanny for my daughter is more urgent than ever."

His eyes softened when he talked about his mom and daughter, making him even more attractive than before. I mentally shook myself, trying to overcome his magnetic pull. "I'm sorry to hear about your mom."

"Thanks." He flashed me another smile before getting down to business. "The agency sent your resume over. I noticed that up until a couple months ago you were studying to become a physical therapy assistant. Have you decided not to continue with that? Because the hours I'd need you to be available aren't conducive to a full, or even part-time, course load."

"No, I decided that it wasn't for me so I won't be going back."

"What made you decide to try nannying?"

"I love kids," I blurted out awkwardly. "I mean, I've always been good with children. I started babysitting when I was twelve, volunteered at the church's day care all throughout high school, and had planned to focus on pediatric patients as a PTA."

"You only spent a year at college. I'm hoping whomever I hire will stay for at least several years. Sophia is only six and will most likely grow attached to her nanny. I don't want to make any unnecessary changes to her routine once it's settled."

Finding the right words to explain was difficult. None of my friends or the few boys I'd tried dating in high school understood where I was coming from. It had to be done, though, so I forced the words out of my mouth. "Leaving school the way I did probably makes me seem flaky, but I swear I'm not. It just wasn't right for me, it wasn't what I'm really looking for in life. It might make me sound old-fashioned, but what I really see myself doing is being a wife and mother. Since I haven't found the right guy for me yet, being a nanny makes sense. I can't promise to stay on as Sophia's nanny forever, but I can tell you that I'm loyal. I'll probably grow as attached to her as she will to me, and it would be hard to leave her."

"You're hired."

I felt my jaw drop as I leaned towards him. "But you haven't even checked my references or anything," I sputtered.

"I'm not used to anyone questioning my decisions." His tone held a trace of steel mixed with humor, so it was hard to tell if he liked that I was questioning him, or if I should never do it again. "But, of course, the offer is subject to the background check I'll run on you."

Since I'd always been one to follow the rules, I didn't have to worry he'd uncover anything and shrugged my shoulders.

"I'd like you to come back to meet Sophia tomorrow, after I've had the chance to talk with her about you."

"That will be fine," I agreed.

"And then, if all goes well, I'll want you to move in this weekend when I'm available to help."

"Move in?" I gasped. "I didn't realize this was for a live-in position."

"It is now." Some of my shock must have shown on my face. "No need to worry, though. Not only will we have my daughter to act as a chaperone, but my mother lives upstairs."

I didn't understand exactly what he meant about the position only now being a live-in one, but I found myself agreeing anyway. It looked like I'd found the nanny position I'd wanted, only it was more than I'd bargained for.

Chapter 2

Nic

"Caduto dalle Nuvole," I muttered softly. The expression of surprise had slipped from my lips involuntarily when I opened up my front door to find the most beautiful woman I'd ever seen. Not in the traditional sense, like a tall, Barbie-shaped model. This woman was all curves and sweetness—a combination so sexy, I was suddenly fighting to keep from scaring her away with an obvious erection. I suddenly had a strong hatred for long sleeve sweaters with buttons up the front. Her dark hair, green eyes, and olive skin hinted at an Italian heritage, and I filed that away for later.

In a spilt-second, I had no doubt the woman was mine. I'd taken her hand and walked her back to my office for an "interview." It seemed the wisest course of action at the moment. I didn't want to scare her away. Not that I would let her go. In fact, when she spoke about her desire to be a wife and mom, I decided to move her in with us. Surprisingly, it hadn't taken much convincing, and I'd had to stifle a lascivious grin when I realized she was just as affected by me as I was by her.

I took her hand once again, helping her up from her seat and guiding her to the front door. I lifted her hand and brushed my lips over the silky skin on the back.

"Until tomorrow, mia dolce."

Anna's eyes were wide and a little bewildered, as she nodded then turned to slowly descend the stairs leading to my front door. When she reached the sidewalk, she looked back to where I was standing, leaning against the doorframe, watching her. I smiled and winked, immensely pleased with the pink tinge that appeared on her cheeks. Damn, she was fucking gorgeous, and I couldn't wait to get another look at the lushness beneath her sweater and learn just how far down she would blush when I was worshipping her body. And make no mistake, it would be happening soon.

I wasted no time calling the agency and informing them of the status change to live-in and asked for her background check to be faxed over. It was in my hands less than ten minutes later. I raised a brow at the name printed across the top confirming my suspicions as to her genealogy.

Gianna.

The name suited her. It was every bit as exquisite as she was. Why in the world would she use Anna? It occurred to me then, she was *my* Gianna and mine alone, while everyone else got Anna. I shifted in my seat, uncomfortably, my cock definitely loving the idea.

"Daddy!" A sweet voice rang out as a blur of tiny arms and legs, with dark hair streaming out behind, hurled themselves into my arms.

I stood just in time to catch her up and twirl her around. "How's my preziosa today?" I asked Sophia as I smacked a kiss on her plump little cheek.

She giggled and returned the gesture. "I'm feeling good today, can I go to the park?" She blinked her long lashes at me, her light brown eyes wide and begging. "Please?"

How could anyone ever deny this precious girl anything? I checked my watch, I didn't have another meeting until later in the evening. "Why not?" Her whole face lit up with her smile, and I felt like the king of the world. I would do whatever it took to see that smile on her face, always. Days like those, they almost made me forget the ones where her perfect face was gaunt and pale, her whiskey-colored eyes full of pain.

We collected my mother from her apartment on the fifth floor of our townhouse. I'd built it for her two years before when my father passed. Knowing she was aging, and eventually the stairs would be too much, I had an elevator installed, which was a blessing for Sophia, who often didn't have the stamina for the stairs, as well.

Our home was in Central Park West, so we only had to cross the street to step out of the concrete jungle and into the lush, green, peaceful atmosphere of the park. My mother and I settled on a bench to watch Sophia as she played on the jungle gym.

"How did the interview go, Niccolo?" she inquired.

I wasn't sure how to answer, but honesty seemed the best policy, especially when it came to my mother. Nobody in the family could ever get away with lying to Mamma Allegra. "I hired her. But, she won't be Sophia's nanny for long."

Mother started chortling, and I glanced her way quizzically.

"Just like your father, aren't you Niccolo?"

"I appreciate the compliment, Mamma, but would you mind sharing the joke?"

She reached over and patted my hand. "Your papà
took one look at me and the next day he'd arranged a marriage with my father. Our fathers were certainly happy for the alliance, but it wouldn't have mattered to my Lorenzo. He would have stolen me away if they hadn't given their permission. Lucky for him, I'd been mooning after him from afar and was all too happy to let him sweep me off my feet."

I knew my parents had an arranged marriage of sorts and they'd been deeply in love as long as I could remember, but I didn't know the rest of the story. "You didn't know Papà before he asked for your hand?"

She shook her head. "He worked for his family, and I only saw him when he came to our house for business. I wasn't supposed to be anywhere around, but once I caught a glimpse of him, I hovered in the background every time he was there." She laughed again softly, but her eyes saddened. "I miss him every day." She pinned me with a stare. "If she is the one, don't let her get away, Niccolo."

"She is and I won't," I stated firmly. "She'll be back to meet Sophia tomorrow. Then I'm moving her in this weekend."

"Into her own room?" my mother asked suspiciously. Raised in a devoutly Catholic, Italian family, she wouldn't approve of my sharing a bed with a woman, much less a room before we were married. I had no such qualms and, while I deeply respected my mother, it was my house, my rules.

"For now." I hated to disappoint my mother, but I was determined to have Gianna permanently in my bed by the end of the next week.

We spent an hour at the park then I took my girls home, instructing my mother to rest and let me order pizza. As expected, she was appalled that we would eat pizza she hadn't cooked. I looked pointedly at her broken arm, and she huffed but acquiesced.

While they ate and watched a movie, I returned to my office for a conference call.

"Niccolo, you're going to have to take over the reins soon, I'm getting too old for this shit," said my uncle, Antonio.

When my father died, Sophia was extremely sick and I was only twenty years old. I asked my father's older brother to step in for him until I was ready to take his place. Antonio had never had any desire to lead the family business. He'd been happy running the front business, the perfectly spotless and legit shipping company. But, he had understood and agreed.

Two years later, he was reminded why he never wanted to be in my father's shoes and he'd been after me to take his place. I knew my time was running out. But now, more than ever, I needed a little more time. I couldn't take over until Gianna was officially mine. I wanted a ring on her finger and a baby in her belly before she found out about my "real" job. I'd ease her into the life before opening her eyes to it all.

"I met someone, Antonio," I stated quietly. There was a beat of silence.

"Serious?" he asked.

"She's mine. Even if she doesn't know it yet."

Antonio chuckled. "There is so much DeLuca in you, Nic. All right, I know it won't be long then. I'll give you some more time."

"Thanks. I'll see you next Friday at the meeting with the O'Reilly's." A snitch we had in our pocket had recently brought it to our attention that a local faction of the Irish mob had been trying to inch in on our territory. We were going to attempt a peaceful resolution first, but I knew this group, and I didn't foresee it happening without force. If things didn't go well, I'd have to hire security for Gianna and Sophia.

The doorbell rang and Sophia perked up from where she was coloring at the kitchen table. I waved at her to stay put while I went to answer the summons.

I didn't realize how tense I'd been until I saw Gianna standing on the porch. She looked nervous but excited, and it was cute as hell. I swept my eyes down her succulent body, taking in the swell of her ample tits, pressing against the fabric of her white blouse. Her tiny waist, full hips, and long legs (despite her height which her bio had listed as five foot five) enhanced the flirty red skirt she was wearing. I glared a little at the hem, willing it to grow longer.

When my eyes returned to hers, her cheeks were pink and my body tingled with the anxious need to drag her into me and kiss the fuck out of her.

"Gianna," I greeted calmly, masking the arousal and need humming in my body. Damn, she was gorgeous.

Her eyebrows shot up at the use of her full name. "It's Anna," she corrected as she moved to enter. I turned to the side but stayed in the entrance, forcing her to brush by me. The touch was too much. I gripped her hand and dragged her around the nearest corner. I backed her up into the wall of my living room and grasped her waist firmly. Her eyes flitted around apprehensively, but eventually, the green pools locked onto my gaze.

"Not to me," I told her gruffly. "To me, and *only* me, you're my Gianna."

Her eyes widened slightly, but I only saw it for a second since in the next one, my lips crashed down onto hers.

Chapter 3

Anna

I'd been kissed before. Or at least I thought I had, right up until the moment Nic DeLuca's mouth claimed mine. There was none of the usual awkwardness of a first kiss. No chance for me to wonder how I should hold my head, if I tasted like the strawberry lip balm I'd put on earlier, or if I should part my lips. As soon as his lush lips met mine, I gasped in surprise and he took control. Head slanted to the right, his tongue swept inside to tangle with mine. His fingers dug into my waist, tugging me flush against his body and proving exactly how much he was enjoying our kiss when I felt his hard length hot against my stomach. By the time he pulled away to nibble on my lips, I could barely see straight, let alone stand by myself without him keeping me upright. The pecks I'd received had been from boys, but Nic DeLuca was no boy—he was all man.

Once I'd steadied myself, one of his hands slid from my waist, down to the hem of my skirt. I shivered when he slid it up my thigh, the heat from his palm searing my skin. "Given more time, I could come to appreciate your choice of skirt, but my daughter is waiting for us in the kitchen."

His daughter, who I'd come to meet and promptly forgotten about when he'd gotten his lips on me. "Crapballs."

His deep chuckle made me aware I'd said that aloud and not just in my head. I felt the heat of a blush climb up my neck to my face. He swiped his thumb across my cheekbone as he stared down at me. "Such innocence," he sighed. "It's almost a shame you found your way to my door."

He didn't give me a chance to wonder what he meant by his statement, twining his fingers in mine and leading me out of the living room and down a hallway into the kitchen. It was outfitted with top of the line, stainless steel appliances and gleaming black countertops, but it still looked homey. Colorful drawings were stuck to the fridge, a few dishes were in the sink, and a large bowl of fruit sat in the middle of the counter. I barely took the time to appreciate the beauty of the room, my eyes quickly drawn to the little girl with long brown hair, practically vibrating in her chair at the table as she stared up at us with shining, brown eyes.

"Is this her, Daddy?" she asked, her voice high with excitement.

"Yes, my preziosa. This is Anna." The smile he sent her way, his love for his daughter clear in his eyes, made him even more attractive. "Anna, this is my baby girl, Sophia."

"I'm not a baby anymore, Daddy," Sophia said in exasperation. "I'm almost seven."

"Your birthday isn't for another five months," he reminded her.

"I know," she sighed. "That's why I'm only *almost* seven."

She was too adorable. I giggled at her response and she quickly joined in.

"Oh, I see what's going to happen," he grumbled exaggeratedly. "You two are going to team up on me, aren't you?"

Sophia and I smiled at each other, giggling even harder. Once our laughter died down, I shrugged my shoulders at Nic and offered him an apologetic smile.

"What can I say? Us girls need to stick together."

"Yeah, Daddy," Sophia chimed in. "It's a girl thing, you wouldn't understand."

Her response and Nic's answering growl set off another round of giggles for me, which were interrupted by the ringing of a cell phone.

"I'm sorry," Nic apologized after pulling his phone from his pants pocket and glancing down at the screen. "I've been expecting a call about an urgent matter and need to take this."

"Go ahead." I waved him away, pulling the chair next to Sophia out and dropping down onto it. "Sophia and I will be fine. It looks like she has some beautiful pictures here she can show me."

There was a moment of awkward silence when Nic left the room, but I quickly filled it by asking Sophia about her pictures. "Is this one a kitten?"

"Yeah," she sighed. "I really, really want one, and Daddy said I might be able to get one soon. It depends on what the doctor says at my next appointment. I hope Dr. Declan says I'm all better and Daddy surprises me with a kitten."

"What kind of kitten would you want?"

"A fluffy white one!" Her response was lightning fast, as though she'd given a lot of thought to it. "Or a grey one, but it has to be super fluffy."

"I'll make sure to tell him to only look at super fluffy kittens if you can get one, okay?"

"Thank you," she said sweetly.

"You're welcome, but I love fluffy kittens, too."

"Maybe you can help with the kitten? Daddy said you're moving in with us." Sophia's angelic voice held the slightest note of uncertainty.

"Your daddy thought it would be easier for me to help take care of you if I did, but only if you're okay with me living here," I reassured her.

"Oh, I am!" she blurted out. "But I didn't know if you had a little girl like me at home who would miss you."

I moved out of my chair and dropped to my knees in front of her, taking her hands into mine. "No little girls or boys for me yet. If I did, then I wouldn't be able to move in with you. I graduated from high school a year ago, but I still live with my mom and dad. I'm sure they'll miss me, but they know it's about time for me to leave home anyway."

"My daddy had me when he was in high school when he lived at Nonno and Nonna's old house." Her admission confirmed my earlier assumption about Nic's age. "But we moved out when I was two because Daddy wanted us to have a house all to ourselves. Then when Nonno died, he told Nonna he was willing to share me with her, and she moved in upstairs and we got an elevator."

That was a lot of information out of such a little mouth. I wasn't sure what to tackle first, so I went with the safest subject. "An elevator, huh? I'd love for you to show it to me. My mom and dad's house doesn't have one of those."

She cocked her head at me. "I don't have a mom, just a Daddy and Nonna."

"I'm working on it, my preziosa."

I jumped to my feet and whirled around, startled by the sound of Nic's voice. For a big guy, he sure was light on his feet. I hadn't heard him return, but surely he hadn't said what I thought. The rich, hot, single dad falling head over heels for the nanny, at first sight, was something that only happened in romance novels, not real life. Even if it did, it certainly wouldn't happen to me. I shook my head to clear my thoughts and stepped away from Sophia, who was staring at both of us, her gaze swiveling back and forth while she had a big grin on her face as she took in the determined look on his.

"I'm sorry to say I need to cut our meeting short. I have business matters which need my attention, and my mother is waiting for Sophia to join her upstairs before I leave."

Sophia scrambled from her chair and flung herself at Nic's legs, giving him a quick hug. "Bye, Daddy."

He bent down and pressed a kiss to the top of her head. "Bye, my preziosa. I won't be too long."

"Okay," she answered happily. She pulled away from him and before I knew it, she was hurtling towards me. Her skinny arms wrapped around my waist as she pressed her cheek against me in a quick hug. "Bye, Anna. It was nice meeting you."

"It was nice to meet you, too, sweetie."

She was gone in a flash, racing away, presumably to the elevator she'd told me about earlier.

"That went well," Nic murmured, twining my hand in his once again.

"It did," I agreed as he led me down the hallway and to the door. My gaze landed on the wall where he'd kissed me and I almost missed what he was saying as I remembered the feel of his lips on mine.

"I've reviewed your background check and references from the agency, as you instructed me to do," he said wryly. "Judging from the hug she just gave you, you have Sophia's stamp of approval, too. There's nothing stopping you from moving in this weekend. Will Saturday morning work for you?"

"What about our kiss?" It certainly seemed like something which might stop me from moving in. Didn't it?

He glanced at the black and silver Rolex watch strapped to his wrist. "Any conversation about the kiss will have to wait because I can't be late to this meeting. I can send a car and men to help you with your possessions. Saturday morning at nine o'clock?"

"A car?"

"Yes, Gianna. A car," he repeated. "In fact, use mine now to go home so my driver will know where to pick you up, and I'll have an associate of mine fetch me on his way to our meeting."

Before I knew what was happening, I'd been bundled into the back seat of a gleaming, black town car. When the driver pulled up in front of my parent's house, I realized I hadn't even given him the address. He already knew how to find the house. Which meant there really hadn't been any need for him to drive me home, and Nic had darn well known it. Sneaky man.

Chapter 4

Nic

"Brandon. Wait a second." My best friend since childhood turned from where he'd been headed toward the door and walked back over to me. He was also the man who would step in as my number two when I eventually took over. He stopped by the table and ran his hands over his buzzed, black hair, the short sleeves on his t-shirt displaying his many tattoos. He definitely looked the part of the enforcer, and we used it to our advantage often.

"What's up, Nic?"

I waved for him to take a seat and waited until it was only he and my uncle left in the room with me.

"There's been movement in the O'Reilly organization. Word is, someone is trying to move up in the ranks by taking on the DeLucas."

Brandon ran frustrated hands over his head and blew out a breath. "You getting this from Silas?"

"Among other sources," Antonio confirmed. "I wouldn't put too much stock in it if it were only that booze hound. But, his information is usually correct and when I heard the same from an informant, I knew we needed to take it seriously."

"An informant?" Brandon repeated incredulously.

There wasn't much Brandon didn't know about family business, but the fact that we'd been approached by someone in the O'Reilly family six months before was one of them. My uncle and I were contacted by someone wanting out and in exchange for our help, she agreed to spend some time acting as our informant. We would never have asked it of her, but she was anxious to boot her father out of his place as the head of the organization so she would be completely free of his tyrannical reign when she finally left.

As much as I trusted Brandon, I wasn't willing to risk anyone knowing about Carly. Her position was too precarious and the information she provided too vital. But, with the way things were moving, I knew it was time to bring him in.

"I'm sorry we didn't tell you before now, brother, but I wanted to keep the circle as small as possible. It's Grady's daughter Carly, and the situation is so fucked up, we need your help."

He nodded, aware that being the number two meant he didn't have to deal with one hundred percent of the bullshit, but always willing to help lighten mine and Antonio's load.

"I'm moving someone in with me on Saturday. I'm going to have my hands full with her"—I was aware of the double meaning in that statement, and Antonio's smirk said he was too—"as well as protection for Sophia and my mother."

Brandon's eyebrows shot up into his hairline. "You decided Sophia needs a live-in nanny? Are you crazy? You'll have a full-time job just keeping her away from the family business."

"It's going to be her family soon too"—Brandon's face went slack with surprise—"but you're right, for the moment, I'd like to keep her clear of it all. That's why I need your help. I can't help feeling as though the shit is about to hit the fan. I need you to become Carly's shadow. If you get even the tiniest whiff that she's blown, pull her out and get her into hiding. She's more than earned our protection."

He nodded, still looking a little shell-shocked. "Whatever you need, man. You know I'll get it done." We both stood to shake hands, our free ones rapping each other on the back a couple of times.

"Let me get Gianna settled, then I want you to come and meet her. If I bring you over too soon, you'll scare the fuck out of her," I jibed. Brandon flipped me the bird and loped out of the room, laughing.

"So," Antonio drawled, drawing my attention, "moving her in so soon?" His grin betrayed his lack of surprise.

"Mamma isn't happy about the sleeping arrangements, but she'll have to live with it until I get Gianna to marry me."

This time, he did register a little shock. "You're moving her into your room?"

"Not on Saturday," I explained. "But, I fully intend to get her pregnant as soon as possible, so those arrangements won't last long."

Antonio burst out laughing. "Such a DeLuca," he muttered through his guffawing.

I shrugged with a grin. "So they tell me."

I stopped abruptly and stared at the most perfect ass in the world. Gianna was bent over, putting a few things in a bottom drawer of the oak dresser in her new room. All day, I'd been forced to endure the sight of her long legs in skin-tight yoga pants and a t-shirt that kept slipping off of her shoulder to reveal a lemon yellow bra strap. I'd forced down the need to punch everyone else who got a glimpse of her creamy skin.

We had just finished unloading the last of her boxes, and I'd come up to make sure she was settling in all right. My eyes strayed to the queen size bed on the far wall, it was a far cry from the oversized king in my bedroom, but it was still tempting as hell. Especially since Sophia was spending the night with her Nonna.

"Gianna."

She yelped, jumping to her feet and spinning around. Her hand flew to her chest, drawing my attention to her incredible tits as they lifted and fell with her rapid breathing.

"Jiminy Crickets, Nic! You scared the heck out of me!"

I chuckled and shook my head as I prowled toward her. She was too fucking adorable and I never wanted her to change. Well, with the exception of bringing out the inner tigress I knew would be there in the bedroom.

Her eyes widened to saucers as I closed in on her, but she didn't back away or break eye contact. Her pink little tongue darted out to wet her lips, and I was fucking gone. Slipping my hands around her waist I pulled her flush against my body.

"You tempt me beyond all reason, mia dolce." I lowered my head to place my lips gently on her neck and my hands traveled farther down until I cupped her round ass in my palms. "I didn't like everyone seeing what is for my eyes only, Gianna," I murmured, nipping at her skin. She shuddered with a gasp, and I smiled as I ran my nose up to her ear.

"Y-yours?" she questioned.

I clenched my hands tight and shoved my pelvis into her, showing her just how much I wanted her. "Yes, Gianna. Mine," I growled. "I think these...pants"—I said the word with derision—"need to be disposed of."

Leaning back a little, I scanned her face to gauge her reaction to my blatant claim on her. I would slow down if I needed to, however, there was no way I was letting her go. She looked a little dazed, but her mossy-green eyes were swirling with desire. Yes, my sweet Gianna wanted me every bit as much as I craved her.

This time, when my head bent down, I brushed my lips over hers, before running my tongue along the seam of her lips. Her little gasp gave me my opening and I plunged my tongue into the warm recesses of her mouth. Just thinking about how much hotter her pussy would be around my cock had the zipper of my jeans digging into my erection.

My hands still firmly on her ass, I lifted her and set her on the dresser, moving to stand between her legs. Our mouths danced, our moans the only sounds in the otherwise quiet room. I was ready to take her right then, to sink myself deep inside her pussy, and hopefully, leave her with a little part of me. Except, if I was right, she was an innocent, and I knew she wouldn't be ready yet.

"Baby," I whispered between kisses. "Tell me something."

Un-melding our mouths, I watched her expression as I asked, "Are you a virgin?"

Her cheeks tinged pink and she looked down, refusing to meet my eyes. I loved seeing that flush on her skin. It was sexy as hell. But, I wanted her to know there was nothing to be embarrassed about. I put a finger under her chin and lifted her gaze to meet mine, smiling gently.

"I want you either way, mia dolce. But, if you are untouched, it would be the greatest gift you could give me, until you're round with my baby."

Gianna looked shell shocked at my words for a moment, but then her whole face lit up like the sun. She looked amazing, and it took all of my control to remain still and finish our conversation.

"Yes," she answered shyly.

A rush of possessiveness washed over me and I growled as I took her lips once again. I began to kiss my way down to the wide collar of her shirt and tugged it down easily, revealing her lacy, yellow bra. It seemed a reflection of her innocence and for a split-second, doubt entered my mind, wondering if it would be ruined by the truth of who I was.

The beautiful sight before me swept the worry away as fast as it had come. I hungrily looked my fill at her full tits, almost too big for the bra. Sliding my hands up her torso and over to her chest, I covered them with my palms. Then, moving them southward, I dragged the cups down with them and her pink nipples appeared, puckered and ready for my mouth. Bending my knees slightly, I put myself at eye level with those delicious peaks and licked around one before sucking it into my mouth.

Gianna moaned and melted into me, her hands delving into my hair and holding my head at her breast. I nipped and sucked until she was wiggling restlessly, her knees squeezing just above my hips. After giving her other nipple the same attention, I placed a tiny kiss on each tip and started to move southward once again, ending on my knees before her.

It wasn't time to take her yet, but I needed a taste to hold me over. I was without patience, so I gripped the fabric on either side of the seam covering her pussy and yanked until it came apart with a loud rip. Gianna made a small sound of surprise, but didn't protest. My mouth watered at the sight of her matching yellow panties.

Sliding the lace aside, I grunted at the glistening lips of her pussy. "Look how wet you are, baby. I bet you taste like heaven."

She mewled and her legs instinctively widened, bringing a smirk to my face. My girl was begging for it, and I wasn't going to disappoint her. Leaning in, I took a long, slow lick, lapping at her juices, satisfied when she became even wetter and a loud moan slipped out.

I looked up to find her watching me intently, ratcheting up my desire. "Put your palms behind you and lean back, mia dolce. Open these gorgeous legs wide for me." She did as she was told and it bared her neatly trimmed pussy even more.

Using my palms, I pushed her legs even wider, moving in closer and using my broad shoulders to keep her open to me. With my thumbs, I parted her lips and all the blood in my body rushed to my cock. It began to pulse, each beat a threat that I could come at any moment. I closed my eyes and did my best to calm down. Re-opening them, I put my face into the apex of her thighs and inhaled deeply. She smelled like sugar, as sweet as she tasted.

I dove in and ate at her, a mix of shallow and deep licks, nibbles, and thrusting my tongue inside her. Within minutes, she was crying out, her body tensed and humming with energy. A glance up at her face and the confusion there, a little fear among the acute look of pleasure, reminded me to tread carefully. This was all new to her.

I placed a soft kiss on her inner thigh and blew lightly on her drenched sex. "Don't be afraid, mia dolce. Just let it happen. This is only the beginning of the pleasure I'll show you." I eased a finger inside her, groaning at the tightness there. When I felt resistance, I stopped, a growl ripping from me as I imagine plunging through it with my cock and making her fully mine. "I can't wait to pop this sweet cherry, to thrust so deep in you, we'll be one, and to spill myself inside you unprotected."

Gianna was lost to me by that point—her head thrown back, cries of passion falling from her lips each time I pushed back in. Her little bud was pink and hard, indicating how close she was. Returning my mouth to her heat, I sucked her clit hard, and then bit down as my finger, once again, disappeared into her pussy.

She screamed and her body began to shudder uncontrollably. I used my other hand to continue working her clit as I sat back so I could watch her come. It was sexy as fuck, and for the first time since I'd been a teenager, I exploded in my pants, my orgasm ripping through me as I watched my woman, knowing every shiver, every moan, it was all because of me.

Chapter 5

Anna

Waking up on Sunday morning, I was determined to start off on a more professional footing than I'd spent the day prior. Not that it would be difficult since I'd ended it with my boss's mouth all over my body, and his fingers inside me while I experienced the first orgasm someone else had given me. After he'd ripped my yoga pants and one of my favorite pairs of panties, it was a major understatement to say my first day as Sophia's nanny didn't go at all how I'd expected.

Secretly fantasized about for days? Maybe.

But expected? Not in the least.

I hadn't spent any time with Sophia except to say hello and get a quick hug before she disappeared upstairs to her Nonna's apartment for the day. And night. Nic had prowled around all day like a large, wild animal, practically growling at the men he'd hired to help me move. He exuded a raw, primal masculinity which was impossible to ignore. Every time I looked at him, his eyes were on me. His attention was intense—fierce. I knew I shouldn't let anything happen between us, but then he'd stalked into my room and all my good intentions flew out the window.

I'd never had such a strong physical reaction to a guy. It's why I wasn't just a virgin, I was completely untouched. There had been cute boys in high school, and a couple attractive guys in college who had asked me out. But none of them had the same energy as Nic. He was beautiful. Savage. Completely unashamed of his attraction to me. And he totally threw me off balance every time I was near him. But today was a new day, and I was going to do my best to forget what it was like to have his lips on my nipples and clit, the feel of his soft whiskers on my thighs. His finger inside me.

Darn it! Shaking my head to clear the sensual fog Nic was able to wrap around me by mere thoughts of him, I hurriedly dressed, getting ready to start my day. Pulling out a dress, I longingly looked at a pair of jeans. After Nic's destruction of my yoga pants yesterday, a dress probably wasn't the wisest choice of clothes because it would give him easier access to my body. We were starting the morning off with church, though, and I couldn't bring myself to wear something so inappropriate.

Glancing at the clock, I noted how early it was, brushed my hair, pulled it back into a low ponytail, and swiped some gloss on my lips. I wanted to beat Nic and Sophia into the kitchen, to start this morning off on the right foot by making them breakfast. Checking my reflection in the mirror above my dresser, I nodded in satisfaction before heading out the door. I closed it quietly behind me and crept past Nic's room on tiptoes. I didn't hear any sounds from behind his door, but I didn't trust him not to have an internal radar which told him I was awake and out of my room. Or to be a light enough sleeper to hear me moving around in my room, since we shared a wall. Yeah, he'd put me in the room next to his. I found it only slightly less shocking than the way he'd made me come. Nic DeLuca was going to be a handful.

I arrived in the kitchen without incident and puttered around until I found all of the ingredients and tools to make French toast. I hummed quietly, lost in the comfort of something I enjoyed and was good at. I didn't even notice Nic enter the room until his arms slipped around my waist, causing me to yelp with surprise.

"Morning, bellissima," he rasped, his breath warming my ear. His voice sent shivers down my spine. It was lethal, and completely unfair that a guy who had his looks also sounded so sexy. The sound of him speaking in Italian was enough to make my panties wet.

"Good morning," I croaked, my voice hesitant and unsure.

He nuzzled against my neck. "You look and smell good enough to eat." He nibbled at my skin, making me squeak aloud, before lifting his head to peer over my shoulder at the pan on the stove. "But I guess I'll have to satisfy my hunger with the breakfast you're making me since Sophia and my mother will be down here any minute."

"Your mom?" I gasped, turning in his arms to look up at him in surprise while running my hand down the front of my dress to smooth out any wrinkles I'd gotten since I'd been up.

"No need to be afraid of my momma, Gianna. She's excited to meet you."

He probably meant to reassure me, but his statement only sent my heart racing more. If she was excited to meet me, then they must have talked about me. My face heated at the thought of meeting her so shortly after what had happened in my room last night. The humor in Nic's eyes and the smile tilting the sides of his lips made me want to stomp my foot in frustration. He didn't seem to be worried in the least.

"I've never met a boyfriend's mom before," I blurted out, my hand flying to cover my mouth as soon as the words left it. I'd just called him my boyfriend. How much more of a dork could I be?

Apparently, Nic had a thing for dorky girls because his eyes heated with a possessive gleam. "Good," he purred. "I'm a greedy man and want all your firsts to be with me."

"Give the poor girl some space, Niccolo."

My spine straightened at the sound of the feminine voice scolding Nic. I tried to step away from him, to turn and greet his mom, but he didn't let me get very far.

Instead, he wrapped an arm around my waist and led me over to where she stood.

"Good morning, Mamma," he murmured, bending low to kiss her on the cheek. "I hope you're hungry because it looks like my Gianna made enough French toast to feed an army."

My cheeks heated further, but Nic's mom didn't give me the chance to think about how her son had introduced me to her. She tugged me away from Nic, her gaze sweeping me from head to toe, before a wide grin spread across her face. "Such a beautiful girl."

"It's nice to meet you, Mrs. DeLuca."

"Please, call me Mamma Allegra," she urged, wrapping me up in a warm hug before stepping away and patting me on the cheek. "There's no need to be so formal."

"Thank you," I replied faintly, wondering even more about what Nic could possibly have said to his mother about me.

I widened my eyes at him in amazement at how welcoming his mom was being, as she moved to the stove. "And she cooks!" she exclaimed, helping me to get the food I'd made served up and plates on the table. "More than breakfast foods?"

"Yes, ma'am." She lifted a brow at me and I hurried to correct myself. "Yes, Mamma Allegra. I love to cook."

"I'm so happy to know I won't have to worry about my son's penchant to order take out if I'm not cooking for him and my grandbaby."

"French toast!" Sophia squealed from the door, still dressed in her pajamas. She raced into the room and climbed onto a chair at the table. "Thank you, Nonna."

"Don't thank me," Allegra said, waving in my direction. "Gianna made breakfast for all of us this morning."

"Anna," Nic corrected, practically growling at her.

"I thought her name was Gianna?" Allegra asked, her gaze darting between the two of us.

"It is," I confirmed. "But everybody calls me Anna."

"Except for my son," she murmured, sending him a sly grin before beaming at me. "I understand completely. I'll make sure to call you Anna from now on."

I murmured something faintly, completely bewildered and uncertain as to what it was she understood. Wanting a way out of the conversation, I helped Sophia cut her food while Allegra and Nic sat down. Once everybody had their plates full, I served myself and was about to leave the room when Nic's hand whipped out to grasp my elbow.

"Where do you think you're going?"

"I thought I'd eat in my room to give the family some privacy."

"There will be no hiding away from us like a servant," he grumbled. "You eat with us."

"This is what happens when you don't wait for a lady to be seated like I taught you to do," Allegra chimed in, making Sophia giggle around a mouthful of French toast and easing some of the tension.

Nic stood from his seat and helped me into mine, his hand slipping from my lower back to my butt and giving it a quick squeeze along the way.

"Do you know how to make pancakes with chocolate chips in them?" Sophia asked as Nic sat back down.

I was thankful for the distraction her question gave me and turned all of my attention towards her. "I know how to make all sort of pancakes. Chocolate chip, blueberry, banana. Even caramel apple ones."

"Chocolate chip is my favorite kind, but I'd like to try the apple ones too."

"I'll make them for you soon," I promised, reaching out with my napkin to wipe some of the syrup from her chin.

"Very well done, Niccolo," Allegra whispered, but not softly enough that I didn't hear her. My head jerked up and I caught both of them staring at Sophia and me. Allegra had a look of approval on her face, while Nic looked like he wanted to drag me off to the nearest cave. I refused to consider what it could all mean. Now wasn't the time, so I filed it all away for later consideration, as best I could, while I ate my breakfast.

Nic insisted on cleaning up the mess in the kitchen, so I left him to it while I helped Sophia get ready for church. I lost the battle to sit in the back of the car with Sophia when Allegra insisted it was more comfortable for her in the back seat. I was ultra-aware of both of them riding behind us when Nic tugged my hand off my lap and twined his fingers with mine on the middle console. He only let go after he'd parked the car.

I climbed out while he was helping Sophia and Allegra, earning myself a glare and a growl. "You wait for me to open the door for you from now on, Gianna."

He didn't wait for a response, leading us all into the church. Nic gestured for me to enter his family pew first. I couldn't argue, aware of all the gazes directed our way. He followed behind me, settling Sophia on his other side and his mother next to her. Mass went by in a blur, with me more aware of the warmth of Nic's body brushing against my side than the words spoken by the priest. If I'd been going to confession today, I'd have quite a number of sins to confess. Both in deeds and thoughts.

We made it to the steps of the church before we were waylaid by the priest, who stopped to speak with Allegra.

"And who is this lovely young woman you had sitting with you today?" he asked, his gaze turning towards me.

The priest's question was directed towards Allegra, but Nic stepped between us and answered for her. "This is my Gianna. You can call her Anna."

"You do know he took a vow of celibacy," Allegra chuckled softly.

"Welcome to my church." The priest's attention turned from me to Nic. "I'll keep my schedule as open as I can since I expect you'll have need for me soon."

Chapter 6

Nic

Gianna was a bit skittish for the rest of Sunday, avoiding me and spending most of her time playing with Sophia. I let her get away with it because I enjoyed watching them bond, knowing Gianna was falling in love with my baby girl. Sophia adored her and every time my preziosa smiled, it strengthened my resolve to keep Gianna. She was going to make an excellent mother to our children.

I did my best not to constantly replay our time together in her bedroom. The feel of her soft skin, her cries of fulfillment, the sight of whisker burn on her creamy skin. Sunday night, after everyone retired, I went for a nighttime run, pushing myself until I was sure I would drop with exhaustion. I came home and attempted to cool my body and my thoughts with a freezing shower. But, I was as restless as

I'd been the night before, knowing her delectable body was only a wall away from me.

On Monday, Gianna and I both saw Sophia off to school. She raced to the bus with such energy, I could almost forget she'd ever been sick. She'd been diagnosed with renal artery disease when she was just over three years old. It had been hard to pinpoint the source of her pain at that age, and being a nineteen-year-old, single dad, it had been exceptionally rough. Sophia's mother hadn't possessed a single maternal bone in her body, and as soon as Sophia was born, she took off. We hadn't heard from or seen her since.

But, Sophia and I were exceptionally blessed to have my parents. They were my rock as I was forced to watch my baby girl suffer. Right before my father passed, they performed surgery to restore blood flow to her kidneys and she seemed to be greatly improved. However, the doctors continued to monitor her kidney function, wary of further developments and long-term damage to her kidneys.

Despite her exuberance of energy that day, she'd been more tired than usual lately, and it was concerning me. I took

Gianna back to my office and walked her through Sophia's medical history, routines, and other pertinent information. I threw in facts about myself as well as encouraging her to unknowingly answering several of my own.

After a couple of hours, my stomach grumbled and I glanced at my watch to see it was just after noon. "Sophia's bus will drop her off at around two o'clock." I smiled and stood, rounding my desk to help her up from her chair on the other side. "Come, mia dolce. I'm going to take you to lunch."

Gianna shook her head and stepped back, earning herself a dark frown.

"You don't have to do that. I love cooking and you have such a great kitchen."

I caressed her cheek and gave her a soft smile. "I'm happy to have you cooking for our family, Gianna. But, sometimes, I want to spoil my girl."

She blinked at me, seemingly confused. I wasn't sure she really knew what to make of her situation, yet. Perhaps I hadn't been clear enough. I grasped her waist and tugged her forward so I could wrap her up in my arms.

"You're mine, Gianna. I'm keeping you. From the moment I saw you standing on my porch, fresh-faced and innocent"—I nuzzled my nose against hers and grinned—"in a provocative little dress you hid under a sweater." I bent my head to whisper in her ear, my lips brushing the shell. "Just like you're hiding the tigress inside I know is there. The one only I will ever get to see, the one that I'll set free when I fuck you."

She gasped and her head reared back, her face a mask of shock. But, even after only a few days of knowing her, I was aware of how much I could push her, and my crude words had caused a fire to burn in the depths of her green eyes.

I kissed her, urging her to let the fire grow, to be the temptress I couldn't wait to explore. When I finally forced myself to stop, it was because I was a hair's breadth away from saying fuck it, and taking her to bed. She was panting and her eyes were glued to my lips. "Unless you want that to happen right the fuck now, you better scoot your sexy ass out of this room and get ready to go eat."

She nodded, still in a bit of a daze, and floated from the room. I watched her gorgeous hips and bottom sway, my mouth watering at the sight. I was losing the battle with my patience, I couldn't wait to be inside her and it was going to happen, soon.

After lunch, we decided to pick Sophia up from school and headed home. On the way, I received a call from Antonio, informing me there had been an incident and it needed my immediate attention. I cursed silently at the shitty timing and apologized to my girls as I dropped them at home. After giving each a kiss, Gianna's earning me a giggle from Sophia, I winked at them and hopped back in the car to head to our warehouse in Washington Heights.

When I entered the building, there was shouting coming from the back offices. I jogged back to them and found Brandon, Antonio, and two of our other enforcers in a heated exchange. They all dropped silent the moment they saw me and a sense of foreboding surrounded me.

"What happened?" I asked Antonio calmly.

He scrubbed his hands up and down his face, before looking straight at me, and I suddenly noticed how tired his eyes were.

"One of our shipments was boosted from the warehouse in Queens."

Fuck! It was where we stored our more...sensitive cargo. The items that weren't exactly legal. "How much?"

"Everything from Saturday's delivery," Brandon answered darkly. There was clearly something else behind his anger, so I waited with a raised brow warning him to hurry the fuck up. "It was the O'Reillys," he bit out. "Our driver caught sight of them emptying the truck and hid until they were gone. He called for backup, but we got there too late."

I scratched my chin, then ran my fingers down my beard, as I stood there, thinking. Something didn't feel right. "That shipment was abnormally large, how was it you guys didn't reach them in time?"

Brandon nodded, agreeing with my train of thought. "He obviously didn't put a call into us right away. And—" he broke off and glanced away, his face darkening with a ferocious scowl.

"And," I prompted.

"Carly knew about the shipment."

I was sure most people's instinct would have been to immediately accept her as the guilty party, but I found it hard to believe she would lift a finger to help her family in any way after what she'd shared with me about her childhood. "It wasn't Carly," I stated, my tone of voice deadly. I was not to be questioned and they knew it. I pointed at the other two men in the room. "You two, get your ears to the ground and find out where the fuck our cargo is." I stared at them with laser focus, my voice now full of warning. "Get it back and make sure they know what happens to people who try to fuck with us."

They murmured their agreement and exited the room, leaving the three of us. I faced Brandon, my expression conveying the seriousness of what I was about to say. "You need to accept it when I tell you it wasn't Carly, and if you can't, keep it to yourself and do what I tell you. Capisci?"

"Yeah," he muttered and stalked to the door, but stopping before he was in the hall and turning back. "Why didn't you warn me what a pain in the ass she is, stronzo?" Then he spun around and was gone.

I might have laughed if our situation weren't so dire. I knew what was coming and it was time to stop putting it off.

"We look weak, Nic. I'm not meant for this and they know it."

I sighed and faced my uncle. "I know. I'm sorry I've put you in this position. You're right, it's time I stepped into my place as the head of this family."

Antonio's eyes shone with pride, and it made me feel like a son of a bitch for wishing he would continue to lead in my place for just a little while longer. Now that I'd met Gianna, it would be even more of a struggle to hide the nature of my business, who and what I really am, from her until she was tied to me forever.

"Your father would be proud of you, Nic. The man you've become, the wonderful father, and"—he winked at me—"the husband you are surely about to be." He walked over and clapped me on the back as he strolled to the door. "I'll call a meeting for tomorrow night. We don't have any runs scheduled and most everyone will be able to attend."

I went home with the weight of the world on my shoulders and yet, I realized a part of me was ready. It was time to do my duty and lead.

Over the next few days, I was incredibly busy with the transition. I found time to spend with Sophia and Gianna, but it wasn't as much as I would have liked. I had hoped to have convinced Gianna to move into my room by then, but all I'd been able to accomplish were stolen moments with hot kisses and some heavy petting. I'd made her come a couple of times, but it wasn't enough. The stress of my work had me needing her more than ever. I longed to sink inside her heat and lose myself to her entirely.

Finally, on Friday, our shipment was located and the goons who'd stripped the truck were made an example of. Their bodies were delivered to the O'Reillys as a message. I knew this meant we were likely to end up in a war, but we would be vulnerable without a show of strength and power.

As we waited for the next move, I vowed to focus on Gianna, to truly make her mine. She'd had enough time to accept what was happening. Saturday night, Sophia would be staying with a friend, and I was going to use every weapon in my arsenal to show her who she belonged to.

Chapter 7

Anna

"I'm taking you to dinner."

It took all my energy to stop my lips from tilting up in a grin at the way Nic asked me to dinner. He totally skipped over the question part and just told me what we were going to do. He was so darn bossy and it had nothing to do with the fact that he really was my boss.

"It's the first night I have free since I moved in. Maybe I already have plans."

"Plans?" he growled, prowling towards me.

"I have a hot date with some shampoo and conditioner," I joked in an attempt to lighten the mood, since he resembled a lion who was ready to pounce.

It had the opposite effect than I had intended. Nic's eyes flared, heating with an animalistic lust. When he was inches from me, he reached one finger out, wrapped it around a long, dark lock and tugged. "If your hair needs washing, I'll do it for you."

I gulped at the thought of showering with him, his hands all over my wet body—mine all over his hard one. It was too easy to picture us together under a stream of water. I leaned into his hand, his fist unclenching, so my cheek rested against his palm. "Dinner's probably a better plan."

"Fuck dinner," he rasped, sweeping me into his arms and heading for his room. "I'll feed you later."

He dropped me onto the oversized king mattress and followed me down. "I tried taking it slow, Gianna," he growled into my ear, making me roll my eyes because the pace at which he'd moved was anything but slow. "I wanted to give you time to wrap your head around what's happening between us, but I'm done waiting. I can't do it anymore. I need you too much, so I'm taking what's mine."

His aggressiveness probably should have been a major turn-off. Instead, my body betrayed exactly how much it aroused me. My heart raced, my muscles went lax, and my lips parted as I struggled to drag air into my lungs. And that was all before he kissed down my neck, scraping his teeth lightly against my pulse point before sucking my skin into his mouth hard enough I knew it would leave a mark. My first hickey. I giggled softly and he growled at the sound, lifting up on one arm to free his other so he could pull my shirt up and over my head. My bra quickly followed and my breasts were bared to his sight and touch. He cupped one of them, rolling the nipple between his fingertips and making it pebble. Trailing kisses down my chest, he reached my other breast and flicked his tongue over the nipple several times before sucking it into his mouth.

"Nic," I moaned, my back arching as I ran my fingers through his dark hair, trying to pull his mouth closer to me.

He chuckled against my skin and switched his attention to the other side.

"Please," I whimpered.

"I love the sound of your whimpers," he murmured. "Knowing I'm the only one who has ever heard them."

There was no hurrying him, so I gave up trying. My hands slid from his head, along his shoulders and back, tracing his muscles as they bunched with his movements. When he moved lower and nipped at the skin on my belly, I bowed off the bed, my nails digging into his skin. I was desperate for him to move even lower, well aware of the pleasure his mouth was able to give me.

Nic lifted up to look at me, and the heat in his gaze made me burn even hotter. I reached down, unsnapped my jeans, and slid down the zipper before I lifted my hips so I could shove them, along with my panties, down and kick them off. His gaze swept over my naked form, spread out underneath him. "I'm the only one who gets to see you like this. Ever."

"Maybe we could move from the looking part of this evening to the doing?" I asked, feeling a little sassy, but a blush immediately heated my cheeks.

"So impatient, my bellissima. But I need another taste of you first," Nic said. His hands were hot as he held my legs open. When he bent over my pussy, I felt his breath against me and jerked my hips up. His hold tightened, and my ass landed back on the mattress. I writhed underneath him, but couldn't move my hips off the bed with his grip on me.

"Please," I begged.

"Mine," he growled, his tongue flicking against my clit.

"Yours," I moaned, trying unsuccessfully to open my legs wider.

He trailed his tongue down one side of my pussy lips and back up the other, over and over again, driving me crazy. He alternated the swipes of his tongue with licks to my clit, easing off each time my body tightened with pleasure. After what seemed like hours of endless torture, he ran his tongue up the middle and drove it inside me.

"Yes!" I screamed, my hands clenched in the sheets as his tongue speared in and out of me.

"Tastes so good," he murmured, sliding one of his hands around my hip and down my stomach until it rested over my clit, ever so lightly. He flicked it gently once, making my hips jerk. When he did it a second time, with a little more pressure, I felt a tightening deep in my belly. And on the third, I went off like a rocket. Nic licked me through my orgasm, flattening his tongue and softening his touch when I began to shudder at the end.

"Holy moly," I whispered when it was over, making him chuckle as he licked along the skin of my inner thigh.

I lay limply on the bed, my legs sprawled, completely naked with him fully dressed above me. "I think you're a little overdressed."

"That I am, Gianna," he agreed, swiftly removing his shirt and pants, leaving him in only a pair of black boxer briefs with a visibly hard bulge. A big enough one that I gulped in hesitation.

"Don't be nervous," he whispered, pushing his boxers down. His cock sprang free, long and hard. Impossibly long.

"You're so big," I breathed.

"I promise it'll fit, mia dolce," he swore, his fingers sliding against my pussy. "You're so fucking wet for me. We shouldn't have any problems. But let me stretch you out a little bit first."

One of his fingers pumped into to me and I whimpered, even while I widened my legs.

"You're so tight."

He added a second finger, working them in and out of me. Stretching me. Getting me ready for him.

"I need to be inside you, Gianna. I'll make it good for you, I promise," he whispered against my lips before kissing me gently. "Give yourself to me now. Please."

"Yes," I moaned.

He pulled away and looked into my eyes. "There's no going back from this. You are mine, Gianna."

"I know," I whispered softly. There was no denying the way he made me feel. This was more than physical attraction. It might be crazy, but I was falling for him. Fast.

One of his hands held on to my hip and the other gripped the back of my thigh. I instinctively wrapped it around him, the other one following suit until I was able to lock my ankles together. His hardness nudged against me, and I felt a momentary panic. Then he was pressing into me. So slowly. Centimeter by centimeter, giving me time to adjust. It didn't hurt, not exactly. I just felt stretched beyond my comfort because he was so big. After he bumped against the proof of my innocence, he pulled back slightly and drove into me with one powerful thrust of his hips. Then it hurt. I felt like he was tearing me in two.

"I'm sorry, mia dolce" he murmured, kissing the tears off my cheeks. "I tried to get you ready. To be gentle. I should have given you more time, but I wanted you too much."

"You're too big," I cried.

"I'll make it feel better, I promise."

The utter sincerity in his voice soothed my heart but did very little for the physical pain I was feeling. I'd trusted him to go this far, so I waited, my eyes locked on his as my body adjusted. After a few minutes, the pain eased to an ache. One which didn't take long to turn into the slightest tinglings of pleasure when my walls unclenched, and he slid deeper inside.

"Mmm," I moaned, wiggling my hips and testing to see if there was any pain. "Feels good now."

"You know you are right where you belong, Gianna. Don't you?" I melted into him. "Tell me you know."

I nodded, unable to speak but knowing he was right. I felt a desperation to be with him that should have scared me.

"I wanted to do this slowly the first time, Gianna. But I don't think I can now. I fucking swear I'll make it up to you, though."

I reached up to rest my palm on his cheek. "It's okay, Nic. Take what you need from me."

He pulled out slowly, watching my face for any sign of pain. When there wasn't any, he slammed his cock back into me with a hard thrust.

"So fucking tight," he groaned. "Perfect."

"Please, Nic. I need more," I whispered, my body clenching against him as he drove in and out of me. He lifted one of my legs and brought it over his shoulder so he could get even deeper.

"Oh my," I breathed at how far he went with the new angle.

He pumped into me, hard and fast, his eyes locked with mine as he watched the orgasm build in me.

"I think I'm gonna come," I whimpered.

"Come for me," he urged me. "Now, mia dolce."

He dropped my leg off his shoulder, and I wrapped it around his waist as he continued to hammer into me. My fingers dug into his butt while I lifted my hips to meet him thrust for thrust. And then I flew over the edge again, clenching against his cock and taking him with me.

"Wow, that was amazing," I whispered when my heart stopped pounding like crazy and I could speak again.

"You're amazing," he murmured in my ear, rolling onto his back and cradling me against his chest.

We lay there together, bodies entwined while we whispered to each other before he drew me a bath. He carried me into the bathroom, easing me into the water, insisting I needed it to soothe any aches away. When my bath was done, I could barely stand on my own, falling asleep as soon as my head hit his pillow. I woke up a couple of hours later, reaching an arm out for Nic, but found the bed empty next to me. Lifting up on an elbow, I found a note on his pillow telling me he'd been called away for a work emergency. It was the middle of the night, his sheets were stained with the proof of the virginity he'd taken from me, and he'd been forced to leave me there alone. He'd seemed more tense lately, stressed about something at work. It must be really bad if it pulled him from his bed at a time like this. I only wished he was willing to share some of the burden with me.

Chapter 8

Nic

"What the fuck?" I shouted as I slammed the door to the warehouse shut. "Someone had better be fucking dying to drag me away from my woman at three in the morning."

"Well then, I guess I better fucking die, shouldn't I?"

My head whipped to the side as two of my men dragged Brandon in through another door. He was leaning heavily on one as he limped forward, blood pouring from a wound in his thigh. I ran over and replaced one of the men, yelling at them to call for a doctor.

We took him to a back room kept for the overnight guards and laid him on an old twin sized bed.

"What the hell happened?" I demanded, grabbing a knife and cutting away at Brandon's pant leg to assess the damage. Seeing it was just a graze on his upper thigh, I sent up a prayer of thanks

Brandon sighed, but when he didn't speak right away, I looked up to find his expression the strangest mixture of embarrassment and rage, it was almost comical. He glared at the ceiling as he grit out, "Carly shot me."

Shock almost knocked me on my ass. No fucking way. "Carly betrayed us?" I croaked.

Bandon's expression got even blacker. "No, she shot me because I insinuated she *might* have."

I shook my head a little, still confused. "Brandon, you pulled me out of a warm bed with the woman of my fucking dreams, so you could tell me you got shot for being an asshole?"

"No, motherfucker," Brandon growled, "That's why *they*"—he pointed at Freddy and Enzo—"called you. I called you because, while Carly was threatening to shoot me for being an asshole, the trigger only went off because someone shot at us first."

Dread filled me. "What happened?"

"She ran away from me. And let me tell you, when I get my hands on her, I'm going to take her over my knee and spank her ass." Brandon's fist slammed against the wall as he finished.

"Bran!" I yelled, "Focus. What the fuck is going on? Who shot at Carly?"

"I don't think they were aiming for her." This was said by Freddy as he opened the door for another man to come inside the small room. The older, balding, portly man was a doctor who I'd known since I was a kid. Doc had been friends with my father, and he was the one we called for injuries if a hospital could be avoided.

"Move over, boy. Let's see what this one is whining about."

I stood to let him by, watching Brandon grumble at Doc for a second before turning a serious gaze on me.

"I was with Carly—don't"—he held up a hand, clearly seeing my intention to question—"we don't have time for that right now." I raised a brow but let him continue. "Freddy and Enzo got to us just in time to see that little fucker Darby running off."

"Would you stop wiggling, boy?" Doc snapped. "You need stitches and I'd rather not sew up your balls instead of the wound." Doc smirked. "Though those may be pretty well shriveled and out of my way. Hear you got yourself shot by a little lady."

Brandon rolled his eyes. "For the love of..."

I was getting ready to shoot someone myself. "Silence!" I exploded. I turned to Enzo, who'd been quiet this entire time, not surprisingly. He was usually more seen than heard. But, this was the reason I looked to him for answers. He often saw more than most and was deliberate in his thoughts when vocalized.

"Explain."

Enzo crossed his arms and leaned back against the door jam, his body only half in the crowded room. "Freddy and I had just come off shift at the bar and were having a drink when we overheard a couple of little shits talking about a reward Pat O'Reilly just put out for the capture of any DeLuca."

Rage boiled inside me but I stayed silent, knowing there was more.

"Darby, his youngest, was hanging with the group, and I saw him sneak out the back. He was packing, so we followed him. I don't know if he knew where Brandon would be, or if it was by chance, but he stopped outside Bran's house and hid in the bushes. There was a pretty loud argument happening inside"—Enzo's eyes cut to Brandon, who scowled in return—"and when Bran came into view, Darby took a shot before we could get to him. He's a piss poor shot and it went wild, but when we heard the second shot and Bran went down, we rushed the house to get to him."

The wheels in my mind were spinning one hundred miles an hour. What Carly had been doing at Brandon's house was a question for another day. What I was most concerned about was the likelihood that Darby saw his sister inside.

"Did Darby see her?" I directed my question to Brandon, anger at the situation and worry putting a bite in my voice.

He nodded slowly. "It's why she took off. She wouldn't listen when I told her it was better for her to stay with me. I couldn't exactly chase after her. She cursed me to hell and back, then hightailed it out of there." He stopped and his eyes darted away, reluctant to continue. I stalked up to the head of the bed and got right up in his face, sick of his evasions.

"Stop fucking around and tell me the rest of it."

"The thing is," he said hesitantly, "she came to tell me about the reward."

"For shit's sake, Brandon!" I yelled. "Darby's probably told Pat by now, and she's out there on her own because you couldn't do what you were specifically told to do and keep your fucking mouth shut?"

Brandon's lips tightened into a thin line, but his expression gave no indication to what he was thinking otherwise. "I'll find her." I stared into his eyes and nodded when I saw the conviction there. It went beyond duty, though, and I worried about what might have sparked between the two of them.

Speaking of sparks, I was ready to get back to Gianna, but I knew I'd be stuck cleaning up this clusterfuck for the rest of the night. Doc finished up Brandon's leg and told him to get some rest, but it was clear he had no intention to follow the suggestion. As soon as he could, he was out the door.

I dispatched Freddy and Enzo to get a couple other guys and put their ear to the ground. I wanted to know everything there was to know about the reward and how far the word was being spread. For as long as I could remember, we'd done our best to keep our family and businesses in a state of peace with the other local gangs, or whatever you want to call them.

Ever since my father died, Pat O'Reilly had been trying to stir up shit between the families. But now he'd gone too far. It was time for me to step up, and considering the fragile state of my relationship with Gianna at that moment, it was just another reason to be out for his blood.

I returned home and silently made my way to the second floor. As I passed Sophia's room, I peeked in and looked at the empty bed, littered with dolls. She was my princess, the light of my life, and now I had another female who was just as precious. They both needed to be protected.

Continuing on to my own bedroom, I padded over to my bed and gazed down at the beautiful woman sleeping peacefully. Her dark hair was splayed behind her and she was on her side, curled around my pillow, the sheet dipping low, showing off the smooth, creamy expanse of her back. I longed to slip into its place but there was work to be done. Bending down, I whispered a kiss across her lips, then went back downstairs to my office.

I started by sending an e-mail to a business associate of mine. He ran a security company and among other things, he provided private security. I wanted bodyguards on Gianna and Sophia first thing. Then I contacted the buyers of our next two shipments and moved the time and location of the sales. I was still working when the sun came up and sometime later, a knock on my office door drew my attention.

"Enter."

Antonio shuffled into the room, mostly shutting the door behind him before taking a seat in the chair across from me.

"We need a show of leadership, Niccolo," he said seriously. "It's one thing to tell the family, but it's time to make it clear to everybody else. We need a response to this challenge from O'Reilly. Make it clear you're not a pushover, and nobody fucks with the DeLucas."

I sighed and passed a hand over my beard, scratching my chin, and thinking. "I'd rather not start a war, Antonio. I don't want the lives of my family, any of them, put in any more danger from my work."

Antonio nodded slowly. "I understand, Nic. But, they are in even more danger if you appear weak."

"Do you have a suggestion?"

He shrugged, a regretful expression on his face. "Unfortunately, that's going to have to be all you. I was never cut out for this, Nic. I just know that it's time to take a stand, and for this family to survive, it can't be me leading the charge."

I knew he was right. I was going to have to be extremely careful and strategic if I wanted to keep the peace.

"Have you told her yet?" Antonio's voice wasn't reproachful, merely curious, but guilt creeped in anyway.

"No. I really can't avoid it any longer. With everything being such a clusterfuck, she's bound to find out and I want her to hear it from me." My voice hardened with resolve. "I won't let her go."

Antonio nodded and opened his mouth to say something but was cut off by the sound of the doorbell. I glanced at my watch and saw it was a little past seven.

"I don't want whomever that is waking Gianna," I said as I stood and walked around the desk.

Antonio got up as well and patted my back when I passed by him. "I need to get going anyway. We'll talk another time."

We entered the back hall, and while I headed to the front door, Antonio went to the kitchen and left through the back door. At the far end of our tiny yard was a gate to a back alley, and there was a side alley one block up that cut through two streets. He only lived ten blocks away, so exiting through the back got him home a little faster.

I heard the murmur of voices from the front of the house and frowned, irritated that the person had woken Gianna. I'd worn her out the night before and she needed rest.

Reaching the front parlor, I recognized Carly's voice. My emotions were at war, one-part glad to see she was okay, and the other angry, not wanting Gianna anywhere near the mess Carly was embroiled in.

I turned the corner just in time to hear Carly say, "The word is spreading about you. But, I have to say, you aren't what I expected. You seem awfully innocent to be with the ruthless, gun-running head of the local mafia."

I screeched to a halt. *Oh fuck.*

Danger

Mafia Ties #2

Anna Martin was looking for a nanny position, but she found more than she bargained for when she fell for single dad Nic DeLuca. When she finds out he's a mafia boss, her head tells her to run but her heart tells her to stay. With his baby girl in the hospital, Anna stands by her man in his time of need. But when danger swirls around them, will they manage to find happiness together?

Please note: Nic & Anna's romance is a three part story, but there are no relationship cliffhangers.

Books By This Author

Risque Contracts Series

Penalty Clause

Contingency Plan

Fraternization Rule

Yeah, Baby Series

Baby, You're Mine

Baby Steps

Baby, Don't Go

Standalones

Until Death Do We Part

About the Author

Hello! My name is Fiona Davenport and I'm a smutoholic. I've been reading raunchy romance novels since... well, forever and a day ago it seems. And now I get to write sexy stories and share them with others who are like me and enjoy their books on the steamier side. Fiona Davenport is my super-secret alias, which is kind of awesome since I've always wanted one.

For all the STEAMY news about my upcoming releases... sign up for my mailing list!

You can also connect with me online on Facebook or Twitter.

Printed in Poland
by Amazon Fulfillment
Poland Sp. z o.o., Wrocław